Tom Sawyer

MARK TWAIN

hinkler

hinkler

Published by Hinkler Books Pty Ltd
45–55 Fairchild Street
Heatherton Victoria 3202 Australia
www.hinkler.com.au

© Hinkler Books Pty Ltd 2003, 2017

Editor: Heather Hammonds
Cover Illustration: Terry Riley
Illustrations: Terry Riley

ISBN: 978 1 4889 3186 4

Printed and bound in the USA

The Author
Mark Twain (1835–1910)

Mark Twain, American journalist, humourist and Mississippi boatman, was born Samuel Langhorne Clemens in Missouri, U.S.A.

As a young journalist covering the American Civil War, he took the pen name Mark Twain; a phrase used by Mississippi boatmen when taking depth soundings.

His first popular work of fiction was *Sid Smiley and his Jumping Frog* (1865). Later came the English historical novel, *The Prince and the Pauper* (1882). That was followed by *A Connecticut Yankee in King Arthur's Court* (1889).

However, Twain's most famous books were *The Adventures of Tom Sawyer* (1876) and its sequel, *The Adventures of Huckleberry Finn* (1884), both of which he based on his early life on the Mississippi River.

Contents

Chapter 1
Drat the Boy!

"Tom! Tom! Drat the boy! Where is he?" shrieked Aunt Polly, pulling her spectacles down and looking over the rims.

There was no sign of Tom in his bedroom, for sure. And that was where he was meant to be at that time of day. But the boy never was where he was meant to be.

Aunt Polly bent down, poking under the bed with her broom to see if he was hiding there. She found nothing except his one-eyed cat, which squeaked and raced out of the room.

"I never will get the better of that boy," she sighed.

Aunt Polly, who had looked after Tom and his brother Sid since their parents died, went and opened the front door and looked out. There was still no sign of him.

"Yoo . . . hoo, Tom!" she shouted.

There was a slight noise behind her and she turned, just in time to seize a small boy by the scruff of his neck as he tried to scurry out of the house.

"What have you been doing?" she asked.

"Nothing," said Tom.

"Then why are your hands and mouth covered in jam? I said I'd skin you alive if you touched that jam. Where's my stick?"

Aunt Polly grabbed her stick and was about to smack Tom when the boy called out: "Watch out, Aunt! Behind you!"

The old lady whirled around and snatched up her skirts as if she was about to be attacked by a mouse. It was all the time Tom needed. He dashed off, leapt over the garden fence and vanished.

"Hang the boy!" she grumbled at the same time as trying to stop herself from laughing. "Ain't that boy played enough tricks on me already? When will I ever learn? Perhaps it's good I don't. When I let him off, my conscience hurts me. And when I punish him, my old heart almost breaks. I doubt I'll see him again tonight. He'll play hooky for sure."

Aunt Polly was right. Tom did play hooky that night, staying out under the stars until dawn. He was barely home in time to help Sid with the household chores the next morning.

"*What have you been doing?*"

But he did have plenty of time to tell Sid about the night's adventures. That, of course, required Sid to do the work and Tom to do the talking.

Sid was a much quieter and less adventurous lad than Tom. Tom was always up to something, or learning some new habit. Just recently he had taken to whistling rather a lot. He had learned some new warbles and trills from a friend. So he tended to constantly whistle his way around the house, much to Aunt Polly's consternation.

As it was summer and the evenings were long, Tom often whistled his way into the fields and far away.

One evening Tom met a stranger; a boy a shade bigger than him. He was well-dressed and wore a fancy blue cap. The boy had shoes on. That surprised Tom, who rarely wore shoes except on a Sunday. The boy even had a necktie. Tom guessed that he was a city lad. His nose was sticking high enough in the air.

"I can lick you!" said Tom, thinking a fight might bring the nose down a bit.

"I'd like to see you try it," was his answer.

"Well I can do it," said Tom.

"No you can't."

"Can."

"Can't."

"Can."

At last, there was silence for a moment.

"What's your name?" asked Tom.

"'Tisn't any business of yours," said the boy.

"Well, I'll make it my business," said Tom.

"Just you try!"

"You think you're mighty smart, don't you? I could lick you with one hand tied behind my back."

"Well, why don't you?" asked the boy.

"I will if you push me," replied Tom.

"With a straw hat like yours, you couldn't fight me if you tried."

"I dare you to knock off my hat."

"Give me any more sass," said the boy, "and I'll bounce a rock off your head."

"No you won't," snapped Tom.

"Yes I will," said the boy.

"Well, why don't you do it?" teased Tom. "You're afraid to."

"I ain't afraid!"

"You are!"

"I ain't!"

"You are!"

There was another brief pause as the two boys walked around each other. Finally, they came shoulder to shoulder.

Tom guessed that he was a city lad.

Tom drew a line in the dust with his big toe. "I dare you to step over that line," he said.

The boy immediately stepped over the line. At last the fight began.

The two boys were soon rolling and tumbling in the dirt. They tugged and tore at each other's hair and clothes, and punched and scratched each other's noses. Very soon, they were both covered in dust and glory.

Tom took an early advantage. Seated astride the stranger, he pounded him with his fists.

"Had enough?" he asked.

"Never!" cried the boy.

The pummelling continued until at last the boy cried out: "Enough!"

"Now let that learn you," said the victorious Tom.

The boy staggered off and Tom turned for home. Suddenly, he felt a sharp pain in his back. The boy had turned and thrown a stone at him before running off.

Tom chased the boy home and then waited at his gate, challenging him to come out and fight again. The boy just stood at the window and made faces at Tom. At last, the enemy's mother appeared and called Tom a vicious, vulgar child.

When Tom finally got back to his home in the village of St. Petersburg late that night, he was ambushed by Aunt Polly.

"Fighting again, eh?" she said, looking at the state of his clothes. "I'll keep you out of mischief tomorrow. You see if I don't. I've got something planned for you, my lad."

Chapter 2
Painting the Fence

Saturday morning dawned bright and sunny –
almost as bright as the tin of whitewash that
Aunt Polly handed Tom. She had decided to
make him whitewash the garden fence. That
would keep him out of trouble.

Tom examined the fence and a deep gloom
fell over him. It was thirty yards long and nine
feet high. He dipped his brush and painted the
first plank. He completed a second and then
sat down to contemplate the agony of it all.

Just then, young Sid appeared with a bucket.

"What are you doing, Sid?" asked Tom.

"Aunt Polly wants me to get the water in,"
he replied.

"If you do some painting for me," said Tom,
"I'll get the water."

"Can't," said Sid. "Aunt Polly says the
painting's your job."

"Never mind what she said," grinned Tom.
"Give me the bucket. I won't be gone a minute.

She won't even know. Now take my brush."

"I daren't," said Sid. "She'll take my head off."

"I'll give you one of my best marbles," said Tom.

Sid began to waver. He was only human after all. He put down his bucket and took up the brush.

Aunt Polly had been expecting this to happen, and rushed out with her stick. Sid was soon racing down the road to the water well with a tingling backside, and Tom had once more reluctantly taken up the paint brush.

Just then, the boy Ben Rogers hove into sight. He was pretending to be the *Big Missouri*, the great paddle steamer that regularly passed close by on the Mississippi River. As he drew near to Tom, he turned to starboard and called out, "Stop all engines!"

Tom knew that Ben would tease him mercilessly for having to work on a Saturday morning. But he had a plan.

"You're a poor chap for having to work," said Ben. "I'm off swimming. Don't you wish you could come, rather than having to work?"

"What do you call work?" asked Tom.

"Ain't that painting work?" he replied.

"Aunt Polly says the painting's your job."

"Maybe it is. Maybe it isn't. All I know is that it suits Tom Sawyer."

"Oh, come now," said Ben. "You don't mean to say you're enjoying it?"

"I don't see why not," said Tom. "Does a boy get the chance to whitewash a fence every day?"

That put a new light on matters for Ben. Tom finished painting a plank and stepped back to admire his work. He added a touch of paint here and there. "Perfect," he said.

"Say, Tom," said Ben. "Let me do a little whitewashing."

Tom pretended to think for a while. "No. No. I reckon it might not suit Aunt Polly. She's awfully particular about that fence, it being right on the street. I reckon there ain't one boy in a thousand, maybe two thousand, that can do the job the way it's got to be done."

"Oh come on," moaned Ben. "Let me just try. Just a little. I'd let you if it was me, Tom."

"Honest, Ben, I'd like to. But she wouldn't let me. She wouldn't even let young Sid do it. Sid was desperate to do it. But she said no to him."

"Oh, shucks," said Ben. "I'll be careful. Just let me try. I'll give you a bite of my apple."

Painting the Fence

Tom finished painting a plank.

"Oh, I don't know," said Tom.

"I'll give you the whole apple," pleaded Ben.

Tom, showing great reluctance and great acting skills at the same time, handed over the brush in exchange for the apple. "Now you be mighty careful, Ben," he said.

So while Ben worked and sweated in the sun, Tom sat on a barrel in the shade, dangling his legs, eating the apple and planning the slaughter of other innocents who might pass by.

There were plenty. They all came to jeer but like Ben, remained to whitewash.

Ben worked and sweated in the sun.

By the time Ben was tired out, Tom had persuaded Billy Fisher to give him his kite in exchange for the honour of doing a bit of whitewashing. Johnny Miller was next. He parted with his toy soldiers for the chance to paint.

Tom had started the day as a poverty-stricken lad. By lunch time he had twelve marbles, a kite, a few toy soldiers, a jar of tadpoles, six fire-crackers, the handle of a knife, and four pieces of orange peel.

He'd also had a very pleasant morning sitting and snoozing in the shade. And by the by, the whole fence, quite miraculously, was soon covered by three fine coats of whitewash!

Chapter 3
Tom Falls in Love

"Can I go and play now?" asked Tom, coming into the house.

"You can't have finished painting the fence yet," said Aunt Polly.

"It's all done, Aunt," he replied.

"You must be fibbing," she said, getting up to look out of the window.

Aunt Polly was quite astonished to see the dazzling fence. "Well I never. There's no getting around it; you can work hard when you want to. Trouble is, it's mighty seldom that you have a mind to."

Aunt Polly said Tom could go off and play. "And make sure you're back before the end of the month," she added, with a smile.

Tom was over the fence and gone in moments. There was a gate, but he rarely used it. Clambering over the fence was much more fun. He hurried over to his friend Bill Harper's house. It was here only recently that a major military battle had taken place between two armies. Tom was general of one of those armies. Bill Harper was general of the other.

These two great commanders did not lower themselves by actually fighting. The smaller fry did that, while Tom and Bill sat on the hill together, conducting the campaign. It was the younger boys in the village who did the fighting.

Those same armies were quickly drawn up again that day and battle commenced. Once more Tom was victorious. Prisoners were exchanged, surrender terms were negotiated and Tom set off home again.

He was passing a house when he spotted a girl in the garden. He hadn't seen her before. Then he realised that it must be Becky, the daughter of Judge Thatcher who had just moved to St. Petersburg. Becky was a beautiful blue-eyed creature, with blond hair plaited into two long braids.

The so-recently crowned victor of the battlefield fell for Becky without firing a shot. Suddenly, his heart was emptied of all the girls he had ever loved, including pretty Amy Lawrence, who he'd only fallen in love with the week before. Now he was ready to worship the new girl.

The younger boys did the fighting.

Tom pretended he had not seen her as he began to show off. He did some dangerous gymnastic twists and turns over the garden wall. Alas, she appeared not to notice him. Then Becky turned to go back into the house. She was almost inside when she picked a pansy from a flower bed and threw it over the wall, before closing the door behind her.

Had she seen him? Had she thrown the flower for him to pick up? Tom dashed over and picked it up. It was in his button hole in no time at all. He stayed by the wall all evening, hoping she was watching him from the window.

He did some more somersaults over the wall and hopped along the top of it on one leg. He even balanced a straw on his nose for several minutes. But the girl didn't reappear that night. Nevertheless, his spirits were so high when he got home that Aunt Polly wondered what had got into the child.

Over the new few days, Tom skulked around Becky's house. But she seemed to have disappeared. Poor Tom was so sad. He forsook his friends and sought solace in lonely places. He found a log raft one day and took to the water, his fading pansy hanging limply from his rough shirt.

Had she seen him?

It was dark by the time he got home, after having decided not to throw himself into the river to prove his love for Becky. He stopped by her house and walked over to a window. The shadow of a candle flickered behind the curtain.

Tom lay down on the grass with his hands, now clasping the flower across his breast. That was how he was going to die of love, he decided. And that's how she would find him when she came out the next morning. He imagined how she would drop a single tear on his lifeless body.

Suddenly, the window shot up. Two hands holding a bowl of water emerged. A deluge of waste water drenched the heroic lover.

Tom leapt up with a cry and a snort, and jumped back across the wall before running for home.

Chapter 4
Tom Loses a Tooth

Sunday was the one day of the week when Tom cleaned himself up, or rather more accurately, when Aunt Polly or his cousin Mary cleaned him up. A few drops of water were all that Tom wanted. But Mary always insisted on a drenching of soap and water.

"Water won't hurt you," she'd say.

She gave his hair its weekly brushing too.

Then out came the Sunday clothes. The Sunday suit was old, but it did the job. There was a shirt with a clean collar and his shiny Sunday shoes. To top it all was his speckled straw hat. By the time Tom had put on his shoes, he was complaining at the discomfort of it all.

Fully dressed and polished, Aunt Polly would lead Cousin Mary, Tom and Sid to church.

Church for Tom was a time for business with his friends.

"Got any marbles to swap?" he whispered to Bill Harper.

"I'll swap two for a piece of licorice and a fishhook," said Bill.

"Done!" said Tom.

"Shush!" ordered Aunt Polly.

The minister stepped forward to speak to the congregation. "Now children," he said, "I want you all to sit up as straight and pretty as you can, and give me your attention. That's the way little boys and girls should behave. I want to tell you how good it makes me feel to see so many bright, clean little faces in church, all learning how to do right and be good."

Tom and his badly-behaved friends made sure the rest of the minister's talk was drowned out, as fighting, fidgeting and hair-pulling broke out.

Tom was temporarily diverted by his old love, Amy Lawrence, who smiled at him. But then he saw his new love, and his soul was ablaze again. He started showing off with all his might; cuffing other boys, making faces and pulling hair. He was doing everything he could to win her approval.

The only prayer he made in church that day was that Becky would fall in love with him!

If having to dress up on Sundays depressed Tom, Mondays were worse. That was back-to-school day. One particular Monday he was desperately searching for an illness to keep him off school. As he lay in bed, he thought that perhaps he might have a cold. He was sure he felt a sniff coming on. But he couldn't quite make himself sneeze.

He wiggled his teeth. Yes! One was loose. He was about to moan with pain when he realised that Aunt Polly would take great pleasure in pulling it out. Suddenly his toothache vanished.

Then he remembered hearing the doctor once describe an illness affecting the foot that had laid up a patient for two weeks. He immediately started to groan as he clutched his foot.

Aunt Polly arrived soon after to see what all the groaning was about. Tom said it was his foot. Aunt Polly felt the foot for a moment and dismissed it as nothing.

"But it hurts so much!" insisted Tom. "Far more than my tooth. I certainly can't go to school with such pain."

"What tooth?" inquired his aunt.

Tom quickly realised he had made a mistake by mentioning the tooth.

Fidgeting, fighting and hair-pulling broke out.

"Which one?" asked Aunt Polly.

Reluctantly, he pointed to one at the front, knowing full well what would follow.

"Right!" said Aunt Polly. "Mary, bring me some string. We can't let the dear boy suffer from a bad tooth, can we?"

One end of the string was tied around the tooth, the other around the handle of the open door.

"I promise the tooth doesn't hurt any more," cried Tom. "And on second thoughts, I must go to school today."

It was too late. Aunt Polly slammed the door shut. The string whipped out the tooth.

Pain sometimes brings its compensations. Everyone at school was fascinated to see the gap in the middle of Tom's front teeth. Of course, he told everyone he had lost it fighting a bear in the woods.

Besides, with a middle tooth missing, he could now spit with incredible accuracy!

"But it hurts so much!"

Chapter 5
Huckleberry Finn

Tom had many friends, but none as strange as Huckleberry Finn. Huck, as Tom called him, was hated by all the mothers of St. Petersburg because he was idle, lawless and vulgar. But because of those things, all the children admired him greatly.

Tom, who particularly liked Huck's outcast way of life, was under orders from Aunt Polly never to play with the boy. So naturally Tom played with him whenever he got the chance.

Huck was always dressed in cast-off clothes. They were more fluttering rags than clothes, really. His hat was a complete ruin. His ancient coat hung down to his heels and only one suspender held up his trousers. The seat of his trousers hung like bags.

Huckleberry came and went at his own free will. He slept on doorsteps in fine weather and in the nearest wood shed when it was wet. He

Huck was always dressed in cast-off clothes.

never went to school or church. He went fishing and swimming when he chose.

He could stay up as late as he pleased and could fight anyone he wanted to. He was always the first boy to go barefoot in spring, and the last to puts his boots back on in the fall. He never had to wash, nor put on clean clothes. In short, the lad had the freedom to do whatever he wanted to do.

"Hello Huck," said Tom, on his way to school one day.

"Hello yourself," replied Huck.

"What's that you've got?" asked Tom, seeing something hanging from his large pocket.

"A rabbit's foot," he replied.

"What are rabbit's feet good for?" asked Tom.

"Well, they're good luck," said Huck. "They also cure warts. Bob Tanner was the wartiest lad in town 'til he tried keeping a rabbit's foot in his pocket."

"How do they work?" asked Tom.

"Well, I don't rightly know," said Huck, with a shake of his head. "But Old Mother Hopkins swears that they do, so I'm giving it a try."

"If Old Mother Hopkins says rabbit's feet work, then it must be true," said Tom. "She's a witch!"

Both boys sat down on a grassy bank, and Huck let Tom have a closer look at his rabbit's foot.

When Tom finally reached school he was late, as usual.

***

"Thomas Sawyer!"

Tom always knew he was in trouble when the schoolteacher used his full name.

"Late again!" observed the teacher, Mr. Dobbin. "It's not good enough."

Tom was about to make up an excuse and lie, when he saw that Becky Thatcher had arrived at school for the first time. She had taken her place on the girls' side of the classroom.

"I was talking with Huck Finn," he said to Mr. Dobbin, knowing full well that just the mention of Huck's name would bring some sort of punishment.

But Tom was ready for it because he knew something. Punishment for a boy was normally a beating, followed by being sent to sit in the girls' part of the classroom. And for most boys that was worse than the beating.

"Late again!"

Tom had seen that there was only one spare desk on the girls' side of the classroom that morning. And it was right beside Becky Thatcher. He took his punishment and hardly noticed the pain of the cane as he walked proudly up the aisle to take his seat beside the girl.

A few moments later Tom presented Becky with a peach from his lunch box. She politely pushed it back to him. Tom gently pushed it over to her again. Once more she pushed it away and Tom pushed it back. This time she let it stay.

Now Tom picked up his school writing slate. He wrote a note on it and passed it over. The message was only three words long.

I love you.

Her reply came back very quickly.

You are a rude boy, Mr. Tom Sawyer.

But Tom had seen her face. He could tell she liked him.

Just at that moment, Tom felt the teacher's fingers lock on his ear and haul him back to the boys' side of the room. The whole class giggled. Tom's ear tingled painfully, but his heart was jubilant.

Chapter 6
Becky's Tears

The harder Tom tried to study his school books that day, the more his mind wandered.

It seemed that lunchtime would never come. Tom's heart ached to be free. He used up the time by planning what he would say to Becky Thatcher.

At last the school bell rang for lunch and Tom flew to Becky. That lunchtime in an empty classroom, they talked about all sorts of things.

"Do you like rats?" he asked.

She didn't.

"I agree with you," he said, "but dead ones can be fun, swinging them around your head on a string."

"I'd prefer some chewing gum," she said.

"Would you?" he said excitedly. "I've got some. You can chew it for a whole minute, but you must give it back to me."

So they chewed it in turn.

"Have you ever been to a circus?" Tom asked.

"Yes, and my pa's going to take me again soon," she replied.

"I've been lots of times," said Tom. "Church ain't got nothing on a circus. I'm going to be a clown or a pirate when I grow up. By the way, have you ever been engaged?"

"What's that?" she asked.

"Engaged to be married," explained Tom.

"What's being engaged like?" she asked.

"Well," mumbled Tom, "it's when you kiss someone and promise not to kiss anyone else."

"Kiss?" she said. "What do you kiss for?"

"Everyone does," he replied. "Well everyone that's in love does."

At that, Becky laughed and ran off. Tom chased her and caught up with her. "I've told you I love you," he said. "Now you've just got to kiss me!"

Becky stopped her protests and dropped her hands beside her. Tom came close and kissed her very lightly on the lips.

"Now that's all done with," said Tom. "Now you know that ever after you ain't ever to love anybody but me. We're engaged. So you can't even marry anyone else but me."

"I promise," she replied quietly. "I'll never love anybody but you, Tom. And I'll never marry

"Have you ever been engaged?"

anybody but you. And you ain't to ever marry anybody but me."

"Certainly," said Tom. "And we must also walk to and from school together all the time."

"That sounds so nice," she said.

"It is," he said. "When me and Amy Lawrence . . ."

Suddenly he stopped. Tom knew he had said the wrong thing.

"Oh Tom," she said, "then I ain't the first girl you've been engaged to?"

Becky started to cry.

"Oh don't," begged Tom. "I don't care for Amy any more."

"Yes you do," sobbed Becky. "Why did you mention her if you don't?"

Tom tried to put his arm about her neck, but she pushed him away and turned her face to the wall. Tom tried again with soothing words, but was again repulsed.

Now his pride was hurt and he marched outside in a sulk. He stood by himself for a while, hoping Becky would come out and make things up. But she didn't. He felt as if he was in the wrong, so he decided to go in again. She was still standing in a corner, sobbing.

"Becky," he said, "I don't care for anybody

but you, I promise."

Still she sobbed and Tom begged her to believe how much he loved her. He even offered her his favorite pencil, but she just dropped it on the floor.

Tom marched out, never to return to school that day. Becky ran to the door, but Tom had vanished.

"Tom! Tom! Come back!" she called out.

There was no answer. Now she found herself all alone with no friends. It was her first term at school and Tom was her new, and only, friend. She sat down and began to cry again.

Becky started to cry.

Chapter 7
Body-snatchers!

Tom ran and ran, after leaving the school. He eventually entered a wood and sat down on a mossy spot beneath an ancient oak tree. He felt so sad. That morning he had been in love and engaged. Now Becky had turned him away. Yes, he was wrong to mention Amy, but he hadn't meant anything and now she had kicked him out as if he was a dog.

"She'll be sorry one day," he muttered.

But the young cannot survive on love alone. Soon Tom was thinking about what he wanted from life.

"What if I turned my back on everyone and disappeared mysteriously?" he said to himself. "What if I went away and never came back, ever again? Yes, I shall be a soldier and roam the trackless plains of the West.

"And if I do come back, I shall return as an Indian chief with long feathers bristling from my head. And I shall burst into Sunday school with a blood curdling war cry. Or . . . I might be a pirate. That's it. A pirate!"

Now Tom's future lay plain before him. He would become a pirate and make people shudder and shiver – especially Becky Thatcher.

And when he was old, he would stumble back into the village church, all brown and weather-beaten, and waving his cutlass. And he would cry out, "It's me, Tom Sawyer; pirate and Black Avenger of the Spanish Main."

Yes, all was settled. He would run away from home. He would start the very next day, but first he had to prepare for the journey.

Just in case he felt lonely, he thought he might have a word with Huckleberry Finn. Perhaps he might like to run away too. So Tom went and found him. Huck naturally thought it was a great idea and happily agreed to join Tom.

That night, Tom waited until the clock struck midnight and then crept downstairs. The stairs creaked and a distant dog howled, but he left the house unseen.

Tom met Huck, as planned, in the local churchyard a couple of miles from the village. Long grass and weeds covered the cemetery. All the graves had sunk and the tombstones

Thinking about what he wanted from life

leaned at frightening angles. A faint wind moaned through the trees. Tom thought it might be the ghosts of the dead complaining at being disturbed.

The boys talked little, and only under their breath. "Huck, do you think the dead people like us being here?" asked Tom.

"I wish I knew. It's awful solemn, ain't it."

"Do you think Hoss Williams can hear us talking?" asked Tom.

Huckleberry looked over in the direction of old Hoss' grave. "He might, yet he can't talk back."

"Shhhssh!" whispered Tom. "What's that noise?"

The two suddenly clung to each other, hearts beating wildly.

"Someone's coming!" said Tom.

"It's the devil!" gasped Huck.

A muffled sound of voices floated up from the far end of the graveyard. Now a figure came closer, an oil lamp swinging beside it.

"It's the devil and his friends, sure enough," continued Huck. "Three of 'em. Lordy, Tom. We're goners. Can you pray?"

Tom tried, but his voice was frozen with fear and he couldn't utter a word.

Body-snatchers!

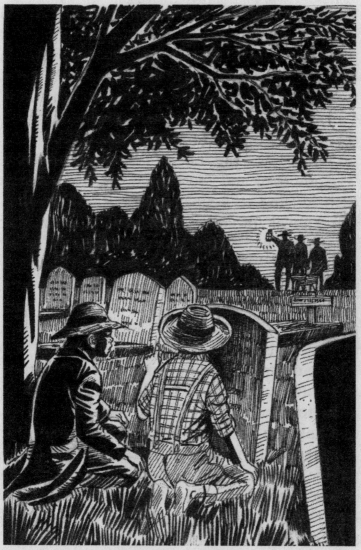

"Someone's coming!"

43

"They might not be devils," said Huck at last. "They're humans and one of their voices sounds just like Muff Potter's. And I reckon one of the others is Injun Joe. If it is, I'd rather meet twenty devils than that murderous Injun Joe!"

The whispers died as Tom and Huck saw three men stop by Hoss Williams' grave.

"Here it is," said one of them.

Both Tom and Huck recognised the voice as belonging to young Doctor Robinson. He was known for doing strange experiments in his laboratory.

In the light of the lamp, Potter and Injun Joe could now be seen beside a wheelbarrow containing a rope and a couple of shovels. The men unloaded everything and then started digging up the grave.

The doctor placed the oil lamp on the tombstone and sat down to watch. He was now so close to Tom and Huck that they could have touched him.

"Hurry up," he called quietly. "The moon will be up at any minute."

Suddenly, Tom understood what was going on. The three men were on a grave-robbing mission. The doctor obviously wanted a body to experiment on.

Body-snatchers!

For a while all that could be heard was the sound of spades at work, digging through the soil. Then Tom heard the unmistakable sound of a spade hitting the coffin with a dull wooden thud.

Soon after, the men put a rope around the coffin and began to lift it to the surface.

Tom and Huck were terrified.

Chapter 8
Murder in the Graveyard

The coffin rose to the surface, and Injun Joe and Muff Potter levered off the lid with their spades. They lifted the body out and dumped it roughly on the ground. The oil lamp exposed the horribly white face of the corpse, which was now thrown into the barrow and secured with the rope.

"How about another fifty dollars for the job, Sawbones?" said Potter, turning to Dr. Robinson.

"I've paid you already," complained the doctor.

"Perhaps," said Injun Joe, "but now's the time for me to get even. Remember five years ago when I came to your door and asked for something to eat? What did you do? Drove me off! Said I was a villain and had me thrown in jail for being a vagrant. Did you think I'd forget?"

Injun Joe now threatened the doctor with his fists. The doctor struck out first though, and dropped Injun Joe to the ground. Now Potter went for the doctor, knocking him down.

Threatening the doctor with his fists.

The two men were rolling across the ground, punching and kicking each other. Injun Joe recovered and got to his feet. He saw that Potter had dropped his hunting knife in the fight. Unseen by Potter, Injun Joe picked up the knife. Then he stalked around the battling pair, looking for a chance to strike.

Suddenly, the doctor broke free and both men got to their feet. The doctor grabbed the wooden headboard that marked the grave. With one blow he knocked Potter unconscious. He collapsed in a heap.

Injun Joe saw his chance and drove the knife into the doctor's chest. The doctor slumped to the ground and died instantly. Then Injun Joe had an idea; a very cunning one. He pulled the knife from the doctor's body and placed it in Potter's hand, folding his fingers around it. He was too busy to see the two boys running away into the darkness . . .

Potter began to stir and moan. A few moments later he recovered consciousness. The first thing he saw was the bloody knife in his hand.

"What's this, Joe?" he murmured. "What's happened?"

"Bad business," said Injun Joe grimly. "It's murder. What did you do it for?"

Potter looked at the knife in his hand again and then at the doctor's body. "Me? I never did it," he said. "Never!"

"That sort of talk won't wash," said Joe. "Look where the knife is."

Potter trembled, and his face went white as he threw the knife to the ground.

"Tell me, Joe," he said. "I've had a few whiskies tonight. I can't remember much. Did I really do it? If I did, I never meant to. Tell me how it was, Joe. The doctor was so young."

"I'll tell it true," replied Joe. "You two were scuffling and fighting when the doctor hit you with the grave headboard. You fell down and were unconscious for a few moments. Then up you came again, and jammed the knife in the doctor. That's the solemn truth."

"If I really did do this," said Potter, "promise me, Joe, you'll stand by me won't you? You won't tell on me, will you Joe?"

"You've always been fair and square with me, Muff Potter," answered Joe. "So no one will hear of this from me. I promise. That's as fair as any man can say."

Potter went down on his knees in thanks and started to cry.

"Stop your blubbering," said Injun Joe.

"Did I really do it?"

"Now be off with you and keep low for a while."

Muff Potter didn't need telling twice. He was off at a run and vanished into the distance, leaving his knife at the murder scene.

Injun Joe now made his escape.

A few minutes later the moon appeared from behind the clouds and shed its soft light on the corpses, the lidless coffin and the open grave.

Chapter 9
Muff Potter Arrested

The two boys raced back to the village, speechless with horror. They glanced back now and again to see if they were being followed.

"Huck!" panted Tom, as they reached the village. "What do you reckon'll come of this?"

"It's murder, Tom," replied the equally breathless Huck. "There'll be a hanging for sure."

"We've got to tell what we saw, don't we?" said Tom.

"What!" cried Huck. "We've got to keep mum. Suppose we did tell and people didn't believe us. They'd let Injun Joe go, and he'd come after us. He'd kill us, sooner or later."

Huck looked seriously at Tom. "It's all we can do. Injun Joe would think no more of killing us than he would of kicking your one-eyed cat. So we can't say a thing."

Tom reluctantly agreed.

"We'll sign a pledge," said Huck.

"We've got to keep mum."

"But you can't write," Tom pointed out.

"You can, though," said Huck.

Tom looked around and found a flat piece of wood. Then he took a sharp stone and started carving some words on it. It took him a while, but at last it was ready. He read out the words:

"Huck Finn and Tom Sawyer swear they will keep mum about this and wish to drop dead in their tracks and rot away if they ever tell."

Both used the sharp stone to prick themselves. Now Tom signed the piece of wood in blood. The he helped Huck to scrawl an *H* and an *F* with his blood.

They buried the piece of wood beside a large tree. Then Huckleberry Finn hurried off to find a haystack to sleep in, while Tom crept home. Dawn was coming up as he slipped back into bed.

All ideas of running away vanished by the next morning, and Tom went to school as usual. But there was nothing to cheer him up when he got there. He saw that Becky Thatcher had returned the peach he had given her. That almost broke his heart.

***

The doctor's body was found later that morning. The ghastly news reached the village at lunchtime. A knife had been found and it had been identified as belonging to Muff Potter. School was called off for the day.

The whole town, including the sheriff, drifted towards the graveyard. Tom joined the procession and was horrified to see Injun Joe walking with the others.

Once at the graveyard, Tom saw Huck was already there. They avoided looking at each other.

Tom saw Injun Joe.

"Muff Potter will hang for this," said Bill Harper, looking at the dreadful scene.

The words had hardly left his mouth when Muff Potter appeared over the hill.

"Get him! Get the murderer!" screamed the crowd.

But Muff Potter was not trying to escape. He was returning to the murder scene. The poor fellow's face was haggard and there was fear in his eyes. He stood before the body of the murdered doctor. "I didn't do it, friends," he said. "I thought perhaps I had, but I'm sure I didn't. I'm not a murderer. Tell 'em Joe."

Injun Joe wasn't going to help Muff, despite his promise. "Sorry, Muff, but a man's got to tell the truth," he began. "You were not to know you killed the good doctor. But you did. It's your knife that killed the doctor and you that stabbed him with it."

Injun Joe even helped to load the doctor's body onto a cart, as the sheriff led Potter away.

Chapter 10
Runaways

Tom's conscience gnawed at his insides for a long time after that. Muff Potter was put in the town jail to await trial. It was a tiny stone building standing in a marsh on the edge of the village. It had no guards, but the sheriff visited it twice a day to bring the prisoner's food.

The jail had one window and Tom often made secret visits to drop off luxuries such as fruit. It was his way of relieving the guilt he felt. But he never showed himself to Muff. He just dropped the presents through the window bars and ran off.

Injun Joe didn't get it all his own way. A lot of people in town wanted him arrested for taking part in the body-snatching expedition. But he was such a frightening character that no one dared ask the sheriff to arrest him.

There was more unhappiness in Tom's life when Becky Thatcher fell ill. She was too sick to attend school. Tom took to hanging around

Dropping the presents through the window bars.

her home, waiting for news. He hoped she wasn't going to die.

Poor Tom. He no longer wanted to play battle games with Bill Harper; nor sail the Spanish Main as a pirate. All the fun in his life had gone. The boy grew more and more sad.

Aunt Polly was a great enthusiast of home remedies, whether it meant swallowing toe of frog or feather of owl. She gave them all to Tom, to try and cheer him up. But nothing worked.

A faint echo of the mischief-maker in Tom did surface when he gave his one-eyed cat a dose of one of his aunt's medicines. The poor creature – it had lost its eye in a shooting accident – greedily swallowed the potion and immediately did a double somersault. Then it leapt around the room, as if it had lost its senses.

Aunt Polly came in just as the cat did another double somersault.

"What's the matter with that animal?" she asked.

"I haven't a clue," lied Tom.

The cat survived and so did Becky. She returned to school and Tom felt better again. He laughed and yelled, chasing boys and girls,

"What's the matter with that animal?"

jumping over fences at risk to life and limb, throwing handsprings and standing on his head.

All the time he kept an eye out to see if Becky was noticing him. But Becky wasn't looking. So he became an even more ambitious show-off. He snatched a boy's cap and threw it on the school roof right in front of her. He even copied the cat and did a double somersault, landing at Becky's feet.

"Oh dear," she sighed. "Some people think it's so smart to show off."

Tom gathered himself up and crept off, crestfallen.

That same day, alone and miserable, he wandered off into the country. By chance he met Bill Harper. "Dear Bill," he said. "I have had enough of life here. There is no joy any more. I'm going to roam the world, never to return."

Now, it so happened that Bill had been having the same thoughts. His mother had just punished him for eating some cream in the dairy. "I don't think she wants me at home any more," he said.

"We shall be brothers then," announced Tom. "We shall see the world together."

A few miles from Tom's home there was a place where the mighty Mississippi River was almost a mile wide. And in the middle of the river was the uninhabited Jackson Island.

That was the spot that Tom and Bill decided to start their adventure. And just so they didn't feel lonely, they hunted down Huck Finn and asked him to join them. He said he would be delighted to come.

It was agreed that the adventure would begin at midnight. They were to meet on the riverbank two miles from town. Tom had seen a small log raft there. It would carry them to their island home.

Each boy agreed to bring fishing hooks and lines, and any provisions they could find. Tom and Bill found it very hard to keep their secret. They kept hinting to others that the town would soon "hear something of interest".

The midnight hour struck and Tom arrived at the appointed spot with a boiled ham and a few bits of bacon. It was a peaceful starlit night and the great river lay like an ocean at rest. Not a sound was to be heard.

Tom listened. Then he gave a low whistle. It was answered by another, and then another.

A guarded voice called out: "Who goes there?"

"Tom Sawyer, the Black Avenger of the

It was a peaceful starlit night.

Spanish Main. And now name yourselves, unless you want to feel my cutlass around your legs."

"'Tis I, Huck Finn, the Red Handed, the cruelest pirate on the Spanish Main," came one answer.

And then a second. "Bill Harper, the Terror of the Seas," announced the last voice from the middle of a bush by the river's edge.

"Give the password!" cried Tom.

"Blood and more blood!" came the answer twice over.

Tom clambered down the bank to join his two companions. The Terror of the Seas had brought a whole side of bacon. Finn, the Red Handed, had brought potatoes and peas, a pot and a frying pan.

The three found the log raft and went aboard. They shoved off with Tom in command. Huck was at the left oar and Bill at the right. Tom stood amidship, issuing all the orders. The craft also had a small sail.

"Bring her into the wind!" called out Tom.

"Aye-aye, sir," replied the crew.

"Steady! Steady-y-y-y as she goes," said Tom.

The vessel moved slowly out into midstream. The runaways were off!

Chapter 11
Camping on Jackson Island

The Mississippi was at low water so there was only a slow current for the pirates to cope with. The Black Avenger stared boldly across the water, wishing that Becky Thatcher could see him now as he faced peril and death with a dauntless heart.

Jackson Island soon came into view. The boys landed about two o'clock in the morning and waded ashore. They hung the raft's sail over some branches to make a tent, and stored their provisions inside it. They were to sleep out in the open, like all good outlaws.

They built a fire and cooked some of the bacon for a very early breakfast. They all said it was wonderful to be out in the wild and as free as the birds. They swore they would never return to civilisation.

After eating the bacon, the three friends lay down around the fire.

Cooking some bacon.

"Ain't it jolly," said Bill Harper.

"Ain't it," agreed Tom. "What would the folks back home say if they could see us now?"

"I think they'd die to be with us," said Huck. "I don't want nothin' better'n this."

"It's just the life for me," added Tom. "There's no getting up early in the morning. No washing. No hurrying off to school."

"Pirates don't have to do anything they don't want to," sighed Bill.

"But what *do* they do?" asked Huck.

"Oh, that's easy," replied Tom. "They have to bully around a bit, steal ships, take prisoners, steal money and make people walk the plank."

"And girls?" asked Huck. "Do they take girls as prisoners?"

"Never!" said Tom. "Pirates are too noble to frighten any ladies."

One by one, the three boys fell asleep.

When Tom woke in the morning, he wondered where he was for a moment. He sat up, rubbed his eyes and looked around. It was a cool gray dawn and the river was still at peace with itself. A wreath of white smoke floated gently above the ashes of the dying fire. Nature was at its most beautiful.

Tom finally stirred up the other two, and soon they were happily chasing each other through the river shallows. They didn't miss home or school at all. Neither did they worry that their raft had floated off in the night.

They soon had the campfire burning furiously again. Bill was about to cook some more bacon when Tom said they should go fishing instead. A little later, they returned with enough fish to keep them eating for days.

Then they explored the island. It was about three miles long and a quarter of a mile wide. At its closest point, the shore was only two hundred yards away. At low tide, they could walk ashore along a sand bank.

They spent all day wandering about and swimming. Early in the evening they heard a booming sound approaching from the north.

"What's that?" wondered Bill.

"Strange," said Tom. "It sounds like a ferry boat. But I know the timetables by heart. There ain't a boat due now."

The noise got louder and louder. They ran to the edge of the island, hid behind some bushes and looked out.

It was a ferryboat. Her broad deck was filled with people standing by the rails, peering into the river. The booming of her engines had stopped now and she was drifting downstream with the current.

"That's odd," said Tom. "It looks like they're searching for someone."

Just then, the boat hooted three times.

"Someone must have been lost or drowned," said Huck. "They always hoot to raise the alarm and bring everyone out to search."

"Yes," said Bill. "They did that when young Jack Turner got drowned last summer."

It was Tom who realised the truth of the matter. "Boys," he said, "I know who they're looking for. It's us!"

"Rubbish," said Bill.

Tom wasn't so sure. He started to worry, in case Aunt Polly thought they were dead.

The three returned to their camp and tried to sleep. As the night deepened, Huck was first to nod off, and then Bill. Tom found himself alone. As soon as he was sure both the others were asleep, he got up.

He went and found two pieces of paper and a pencil in his bag. He wrote two notes. He rolled up one and put it in his trouser pocket; the other he put in Bill's hat. He also put several schoolboy treasures in that hat,

"It looks like they're searching for someone."

including a lump of chalk, three fishhooks and some marbles.

Then he tiptoed away. When he was sure he was out of hearing, he raced away to where the sand bank crossed to the mainland. The river was getting higher and he had to wade across. Safely ashore, he raced down the riverbank and reached the ferryboat station. The boat was still there. Unseen, Tom scrambled aboard and hid.

Tom knew that this particular Mississippi boat was due to leave at midnight. It left on time, and within twenty minutes, the boat pulled into St. Petersburg. As the great paddles came to a stop, he dived overboard.

Within a few minutes he was outside Aunt Polly's house.

Chapter 12
A Midnight Visit

Tom looked through the window. He saw that the parlor was occupied by Aunt Polly, Sid, Cousin Mary and Bill Harper's mother. He crept inside and silently closed the door behind him. From the corridor, he listened to what they were saying.

"Tom wasn't a bad boy," said Aunt Polly. "Just mischievous. He never meant anyone harm."

"It was the same with Bill," said Mrs. Harper. "Always up to mischief, yet he was kind. Now he's gone forever; I'll never see him again."

Mrs. Harper sobbed. Her heart was broken.

"God'll take care of both of them," said Aunt Polly, bursting into tears herself.

From the conversation he overheard, Tom understood that someone had reported seeing him, Bill and Huck setting out across the river on the raft. When the raft was found drifting with no one aboard, everyone had assumed all three had drowned.

Tom listened to what they were saying.

"When will the funeral be?" asked Mrs. Harper.

"If they ain't found," said Aunt Polly, "there'll be a funeral service in three days' time, on the Sunday afternoon."

Soon after that Mrs. Harper left and the others went to bed. Tom waited a while, then crept into Aunt Polly's bedroom. She was fast asleep.

Now, Tom's arrival in her bedroom was what his mission that night was all about. The note he had written and put in his trouser pocket before leaving Jackson Island explained all. It read:

We ain't dead. We're only off playing pirates. So don't worry about us.

Tom had come home to leave the message with Aunt Polly just in case she was worrying they had drowned. But now a very mischievous thought crossed his mind; a very mischievous thought indeed, as Aunt Polly would later discover.

He didn't leave the note. Instead, he kissed Aunt Polly affectionately on the forehead and crept out of the room.

Tom left by the front door and hurried down to the river again. The ferry was moored at the town harbour, ready for its first morning run.

The boat was deserted. Tom got aboard and hid himself again. A short time later, the boat left. Tom waited until it was opposite Jackson Island and then dropped over the side and swam ashore.

It was broad daylight by the time he reached the island. It was Wednesday morning. He hurried across the island, to the camp.

Just before he got there, he saw Bill and Huck talking. He couldn't resist spying on his two friends. He crept up, hid behind a bush and listened to what they were saying.

"Tom's a true-blue," said Bill. "He'll come back. He won't desert us. He knows he would be disgraced as a pirate if he did. He's up to something or other. And I'm sure wondering what it is."

"Well the things he left us are ours now," said Huck. "You can have the marbles if I can have the chalk and the fishhooks."

Bill held his hand up. "Not yet," he said, "the note he left says we can have them if he isn't back by breakfast. And it ain't quite that time yet."

Swimming to Jackson Island.

It was just then that Tom made a dramatic appearance from behind the bush. "I'm ready for breakfast now!" he laughed.

Despite their protests, he refused to tell the others where he had been. But he did say that all would be revealed come Sunday.

A sumptuous breakfast of bacon and fish followed. Then the exhausted Tom fell asleep, and he didn't wake up till evening.

They spent the next day swimming and racing around the island playing pirates. That night they ate the last of the bacon.

The following day they went fishing. But Bill was becoming rather homesick and Huck was getting bored. He liked to be on the move all the time.

"Just one more day," said Tom, "and then we'll head for home. And I promise you I will reveal the greatest secret ever. Besides we haven't played Indians yet."

The other two reluctantly agreed. The whole of Saturday was spent whoopin' and hollering around the island. By the end of the day they had played the best game of Indians ever.

That night, a fearful storm struck the island. Lightning turned night into day, thunder shook the ground and the rain poured down. For

The following day they went fishing.

once, the boys ran to take cover beneath the tent made from the raft sail. Then even that was blown away as the winds roared across the island, turning the Mississippi into a foaming and raging beast.

Tom wondered if the river was angry with him for keeping such a mischievous secret from his friends – and from dear Aunt Polly and the rest of his family.

The storm only relented in the morning. They were all soaked to the skin. But the sun came out once more, and they got their fire going again. As soon as they were dry, they had their last feast of fish and peas.

Then they set off for home.

Chapter 13
Tom's Funeral Surprise

The people of St. Petersburg were in mourning that Sunday.

Becky Thatcher had been crying since dawn. "I have nothing to remember Tom by," she wept. "I wish I'd never given him back his peach. That would be better than nothing. I'll never see him again."

On the Sunday afternoon, the church bells rang out solemnly. By three o'clock the church was full. Most of the village had turned out for the funeral of Tom, Bill and Huck.

Right at the front sat Aunt Polly, Sid and Mary, and the Harper family. If Huck had ever had any family, there certainly wasn't any member of it in the church.

As the service proceeded, the minister said what nice boys they had been. He even had especially kind words to say about Huck. If the minister was to be believed, the three boys were the sweetest, gentlest, most unselfish and loving creatures that ever walked the earth.

His words, hardly true of course, only made everyone cry the more.

At last the minister bowed his head in prayer. A moment later, the main door of the church creaked open. The minister raised his tear-stained eyes, still half hidden behind a large red handkerchief, and looked down to the door. For a moment he stood transfixed. He had just seen three ghosts.

The minister fainted to the floor.

The whole congregation rose and looked back as the three "dead" boys came marching up the aisle. Tom was leading, with Bill next. Huck, looking like a ruin in drooping rags, was sneaking along sheepishly in the rear.

Aunt Polly, Mary and Sid and the Harpers threw themselves on their lost ones, smothering them with kisses and hugs. Huck stood alone, unloved and very uncomfortable.

"Aunt Polly," cried Tom, "it ain't fair. Someone's got to hug Huck."

Aunt Polly was only too happy to share her great relief with Huck. The way she hugged and kissed him only made him feel more uncomfortable.

"Praise the Lord!" cried the minister. "Sing

The boys came marching up the aisle.

out everyone and put your hearts into it."

The organ boomed out and the congregation sang until the rafters shook. All the time, Tom Sawyer looked around and confessed to himself that this was the proudest moment of his life.

This had been Tom's secret. This had been what he had planned, ever since returning home on the Wednesday night and hearing about plans for his funeral. His secret had always been to return home with his brother pirates so they could all attend their own funeral.

"I won't say it wasn't a fine joke," said Aunt Polly afterwards. "But it was rather cruel to keep us waiting all this time, thinking you were drowned. You might have come over during the week and given me a hint that you weren't drowned after all. I wouldn't have minded if you had let me know, and then ran back again to join your friends."

"Yes," said Cousin Mary. "You could have done that. But I don't suppose that thought ever entered your head."

"Tell me," said Aunt Polly. "Would you have come back if you had thought of it?"

Tom saw how much his family really loved him, and a broad grin crossed his face. "The truth is that I did come back on Wednesday night. I was going to leave a note for you saying 'We ain't dead. We're only off playing pirates'."

"You're fibbing," said Sid. "You never came back."

"I can prove it!" announced Tom. "I've still got the note. I can show it to you. But the real truth is that my mischievousness got the better of me. I never left it."

Tom pulled out his note and showed it to everyone.

"That doesn't prove anything," said Sid. "You could have written that this morning."

Tom wasn't beaten. "What if I tell you all exactly what you were saying to each other last Wednesday night? Will you believe me then?"

"Might," said Sid.

So Tom recalled every word he had overheard. The evidence was there for all to hear. Aunt Polly immediately forgave him for his mischief and gave him a few more hugs. And she loved him more than ever when he described what happened when he crept into her room that night.

"That was when I decided not to leave the note behind because I suddenly thought it

Tom saw how much his family loved him.

would be a great idea to attend our own funeral. But I did kiss you before I left."

Now Aunt Polly knew for sure that Tom really did love her.

Chapter 14
Tom the Hero

Tom became a hero when news spread around the district that a very much alive Master Sawyer and his friends had turned up at their own funeral!

Tom didn't skip and prance like a show-off now. He moved with more of a dignified swagger, as became a bold pirate who had achieved the impossible. Smaller boys followed him everywhere, basking in his glory. Bigger boys were consumed with envy at his achievement.

At school, the children made such a thing of Tom's adventure. Tom became rather too big for his boots. He decided that he had no need of Becky Thatcher now. Glory was sufficient. He would live for glory.

Then Tom thought that perhaps Becky might want to make up with him, now that he was so distinguished. Well, let her, he thought. She had ignored him. Now he could ignore her.

Becky did come up to him a couple of times,

but he looked away from her. Soon he saw that she was always dashing around the school, playing games, chasing schoolmates and generally showing off in front of him. The tables were turned.

Becky also noticed that Tom was paying Amy Lawrence quite a lot of attention again. That hurt Becky a lot. Tears came to her eyes whenever it happened. But Becky had a plan. She started flirting with Alfred Temple, a good-looking boy.

Becky took to reading with Alfred every lunchtime. It drove Tom mad with jealousy. Alfred had a rich father and that made Tom even madder. He swore he would knock Alfred's head off if he ever got the chance. He went through the motions of thrashing an imaginary boy, pummelling the air with his fists.

"Take that!" he cried. "And that! And that!"

But just as Tom had soon tired of Amy Lawrence's company, so Becky got bored with Alfred.

One morning, Tom bumped into Becky on the way to school. Tom had by now realised that it was Becky who he truly loved.

"I'm sorry for ignoring you," he said. "I will never do it again. You are my favourite girl. And always will be."

He had no need of Becky Thatcher now.

"Mr. Tom Sawyer," she said, "it's much too late for apologies. I never want to speak to you again."

With that, she tossed her head in the air and walked off.

Tom was so shocked that he didn't even have time to say, "Who cares, Miss Smarty Pants!"

At school that day, he just wished Becky was a boy. Then he could have fought her and thrown her over the school wall! As for Becky, she was about to get herself into trouble with the teacher, Mr. Dobbin.

Mr. Dobbin was a tyrant who wielded his cane at every opportunity. Under his wig, he had a perfectly bald and shiny head. One of the great mysteries about Mr. Dobbin was a book that he kept under lock and key in his desk.

Each day he unlocked his desk and took out the mysterious book to read through a few pages. Then it was always securely locked away again. There wasn't a pupil in the school who wouldn't have given away all their marbles to see what was in that book.

The chance to solve the mystery of Mr. Dobbin's book finally fell to Becky.

"Take that! And that! And that!"

Chapter 15

Becky and the Teacher's Book

One morning Becky saw that Mr. Dobbin had forgotten to lock his desk. Immediately, she sneaked a look inside and saw the book. She quickly pulled it out. It was a text book on human anatomy.

While Becky was busy looking at the strange illustrations, Tom came by and spotted what she was up to. Becky jumped in surprise at seeing Tom, and tried to hide the book. But in doing so, she accidentally tore a page from it.

She threw the book inside the teacher's desk. "Tell on me if you like, Tom Sawyer," she cried, as she started to run off. "I'll be whipped and that'll make you happy."

The next morning, Mr. Dobbin gave the class some notes to read through. With his pupils busy reading, he took the chance to pull out his anatomy book. It wasn't long before he stood up, his face red with anger. "And who is

Becky jumped in surprise.

responsible for this?" he shouted, holding the torn page in his hand.

Tom shot a look at Becky. He could see she was terrified. Suddenly, he felt so sorry for her.

"Who ripped the page?" asked Mr. Dobbin, looking up and down the rows of desks. "Was it you, Ben Rogers?"

The question was followed by a firm denial.

"Bill Harper, was it you?"

Another denial. Tom's uneasiness grew under the torture of these proceedings.

Mr. Dobbin asked each boy the same question. Each one denied responsibility. Now he turned to the girls.

"Amy Lawrence. Did you do it?"

There was a shake of the head.

"Gracie Miller?"

Another denial.

"Susan Harper did you do it?"

Again, no.

"Rebecca Thatcher, did you tear the book?"

Tom glanced at Becky's face. It was white with terror.

"Look me in the eye Rebecca," said Mr. Dobbin. "Did you tear my book?"

A thought shot like lightning through Tom's mind. He sprang to his feet and shouted, "I did it!"

"I did it!"

Mr. Dobbin was furious and punished Tom hard. Yet Tom didn't mind. He saw the gratitude and adoration that shone out of Becky's eyes. That soft, kind look in Becky's eyes seemed to Tom to be worth a hundred floggings with Mr. Dobbin's cane.

It made no difference either that Mr. Dobbin ordered him to stay behind after class for two hours. He knew that Becky would still be waiting outside for him afterwards. And when he finally got out, she gave him her undying thanks for saving her from a beating.

The longer the school term went on, the

crueller Mr. Dobbin seemed to become. His cane was swishing every day. The boys and girls spent their days in terror, and their nights plotting revenge against the cruel teacher.

They took every chance to do mischief to the teacher. But he was always ready for whatever mischief they produced. His own revenge was quick and painful, and came with the cane. The pupils always left the battlefield badly "worsted", as Tom used to say.

It needed all of Tom's cleverness to come up with a plan that promised a dazzling and humiliating revenge over Mr. Dobbin.

Chapter 16
Mr. Dobbin's Humiliation

Tom chose the night of the end-of-term examination results to put his plan into operation.

It was the night when all the important people from the district came to the school, including the mayor. Mr. Dobbin always used the occasion to boast how well he had taught the boys and girls.

Everyone was seated in the schoolhouse, listening as the boys and girls performed poems and readings. Tom recited two verses; the first included some dashing lines about a sailor's bold deeds during a sea battle.

"The boy stood on the burning deck,
Whence all but he had fled.
The flame that lit the battle's wreck,
Shone around him o'er the dead."

Then he announced he would recite a verse from Shakespeare. How that impressed

Tom recited two verses.

Mr. Dobbin! But perhaps the schoolmaster didn't pay enough attention to one of the lines in it. It was one Tom had chosen well and he winked at Becky as he read it.

"Thus the whirligig of time brings in his revenges . . ."

Mr. Dobbin listened with a contented smile on his face. Such eloquence, such learning from one so young. How the mayor and all the other important guests must have been impressed!

But Mr. Dobbin failed to see young Tom creep out of the room. He had urgent business to attend to with Huckleberry Finn, who was waiting outside.

Everyone knew that the evening traditionally ended with Mr. Dobbin drawing a map of America on the blackboard. Then he would ask the pupils to mark various places on it. Mr. Dobbin used it to show the guests how well he had taught the children geography.

Mr. Dobbin began his task, his shaky hand making a very rough outline of the eastern coastline of America. It was so bad that he rubbed it all out and began again.

Now a gentle titter of laughter was heard

from the back of the room. This put the teacher off even more. With his back to the audience, he felt as if the eyes of everyone were fixed on him. But he continued with his task.

Much to Mr. Dobbin's annoyance, the laughter continued, getting louder all the time. Even the mayor and his wife were giggling now. And well they might. It was nothing to do with the map of America. Nothing at all!

Above Mr. Dobbin's head, there was a small hatchway in the ceiling. And that hatchway had just opened. From the opening, a basket on a rope had emerged. In the basket was a one-eyed cat, safely held in place by several strands of wool. An invisible hand from inside the roof space slowly lowered the cat and basket.

The laughter got louder and louder. The cat was now within six inches of Mr. Dobbin's head. Down, down, down. A little lower, a little lower . . .

The room was now in hysterics. Mr. Dobbin, his face red with fury, turned to see what was happening.

Too late!

In a flash, the cat stretched out its paw and snatched his wig, and clung to it as though its life depended on it.

In the basket was a one-eyed cat.

Mr. Dobbin made a desperate grab to save his modesty. But it was too late. The cat was hauled up quickly into the roof space again with the trophy still in its possession. The hatchway slammed shut, but not before the guests had seen a glimpse of two faces – Tom Sawyer's and Huck Finn's.

And how the lights did blaze down on Mr. Dobbin's shiny, bald head! He was utterly humiliated and the dignitaries just couldn't stop laughing.

No one saw Tom and Huck emerge from the roof in another part of the school and scurry away with the cat and wig. Revenge was sweet for the boys and girls. And better still, it was now vacation time!

Chapter 17
Vacation Blues

After all the excitement of Mr. Dobbin's humiliation, the vacation seemed positively boring for Tom. Nothing was happening, so he joined the army cadets, hoping for a chance of glory.

He couldn't wait to wear his uniform and display his red sash. He was pretty certain that the first chance to wear it in public would be at the funeral of the old and distinguished Judge Frazer; not that he was dead yet. He just seemed to be on the edge of departing this world. Such a funeral was a fine thing. And for Tom, who liked to show off, it would be the high point of the vacation.

Tom was hungry for daily news of the Judge's condition. One day the old man seemed to be failing, the next he was alive and well again. At last it was announced that the Judge was recovering and on the mend.

Tom was disgusted and so disappointed that he handed in his uniform and resigned from the cadets. That night the Judge suffered a relapse and died. Tom resolved never to trust such a man again!

Tom was a free boy again. Yet there was no adventure to be seen or had as far as he could see. Even Becky Thatcher had vanished to Constantinople, on holiday with her parents. A circus did come to town, and Tom and his friends played circus for three days after that.

The dreadful secret of the doctor's murder still haunted Tom, as did the sight of Muff Potter languishing in the local jail, awaiting trial.

Then came the measles. For two long weeks he lay a prisoner, unaware of the world and its happenings. He was very ill. When he recovered, he discovered that everyone had, rather boringly, become a do-gooder. Ben Rogers was now visiting the poor and Bill Harper was painting Aunt Polly's house for free!

Tom grew sadder and sadder. Was there no excitement to be had? At last, he sought out Huck Finn. But neither he, nor Mr. Dobbin's wig, were to be found.

That night there was a terrific thunderstorm with driving rain and lightning. Tom had not a shadow of a doubt that the storm was aimed at

A circus came to town.

105

him. The closer the time came for the trial of Muff Potter, the more convinced he was that the gods in the heavens were angry at him for not telling the truth.

The next day, the doctor was back. Tom had suffered a relapse of the measles. He spent the next three weeks in bed.

Tom, who was sure he was about to die, was rather sad when he finally awoke one morning to discover that he had not died of boredom, but had completely recovered.

Out of bed once more, he filled his time with just about any occupation he could dream up.

One day, he set up a courtroom in the field behind his house. He played the judge while Bill Harper and Huck Finn helped make up the twelve good men and true on the jury. They only tried one case; that of Tom's one-eyed cat, charged with the theft of Mr. Dobbin's wig!

Then finally, the sleepy atmosphere of the village stirred. The trial of Muff Potter was about to begin. It was the talk of the whole district.

Every mention of the murder sent a shudder through Tom. His conscience was badly troubled. He didn't see how he could be suspected of knowing anything about the murder, but

Tom's one-eyed cat was charged with theft.

that didn't stop him feeling guilty about the whole affair. It kept him in a permanent cold shiver.

At last, he went and found Huck. "Huck," he said, "have you told anyone about that thing?"

"'Bout what?" Huck replied.

"You know what, that night with Injun Joe and all that," said Tom.

"Of course I haven't," said Huck.

"Never a single word?"

"Never a solitary word, so help me," replied Huck.

"I was just afraid," said Tom.

"Why Tom," he replied, "we wouldn't be alive if the truth got out. Injun Joe would have cut us to pieces."

"Huck," said Tom, still a little worried, "there's nobody that could get you to tell, is there?"

"Nobody! Never!" said Huck.

"I'm sure we're safe," said Tom, "as long as we keep mum. But let's swear again to be absolutely sure."

So they swore again to keep the truth of the dreadful business a secret. But that didn't stop them from worrying about Muff Potter, who was about to face trial for a murder that he didn't commit.

"Have you told anyone about that thing?"

"I reckon he's a goner," said Tom. "He'll hang won't he?"

"Sure," said Huck. "He might be innocent of this murder, yet there never was a villain like him. It's a wonder he hasn't been hung before now. And if he got out of jail, the people would lynch him anyway."

"But I do feel a little sorry for him," said Tom.

"Me too, I suppose," said Huck. "But he's a goner, Tom. A goner!"

Chapter 18
Muff Potter's Trial

As twilight fell one evening, Huck and Tom found themselves hanging about near the jail. The two boys did as they had often done before; they went to the cell window and gave Muff Potter some chewing gum and other treats. By now he had recognised his benefactors.

His gratitude for their gifts embarrassed them. They felt so cowardly and treacherous.

"You've been mighty good to me boys," said Potter, reaching up to the window to collect his gifts. "Often I says to myself, 'All my old pals have deserted me, and I used to mend their kites and toys when they were young 'uns. But they've all forgot about old Muff now he's in trouble. Still, Tom and Huck don't forget'. That's what I says to myself in the dead of nights when I see the hangman a-coming."

Tom and Huck felt awful.

"I know I've done wrong," Muff continued. "I must have been drunk and crazy at the time.

Bringing Muff Potter some treats.

That's the only way I can account for what I did. And now I've got to swing for it . . . and that's right 'cos I killed a man. And I'm going to plead guilty."

Tom and Huck shivered in the chill evening air.

"But don't you feel bad, boys," he went on. "I don't want to make you feel bad. Just keep off the drink and getting drunk. That way you won't end up in here."

Tom went home miserable, and his dreams that night were full of horrors.

The next day Muff Potter was taken to the courthouse where Becky's father, Judge Thatcher, was to hear the case. Tom and Huck were not allowed in the courthouse, but hung about outside. Both kept their ears open as people came out.

After two days, the talk was that Injun Joe's evidence was unshakeable. There seemed no doubt what the judge's decision would be.

The following day, when Judge Thatcher was due to give his decision, the entire village flocked to the courthouse. The court was full when Muff Potter, pale and haggard, was brought in with chains around his legs.

The prosecution lawyer had a few last

Muff Potter was brought into court.

witnesses to bring in. The first said that he had seen Potter washing blood off his hands in a creek, the day after the murder.

The next witness told of finding Potter's knife by the corpse.

A third witness swore that he had seen the knife in Potter's possession.

Everyone expected Potter's lawyer to question the witnesses, and perhaps dispute the facts. But he told the court he had no questions. The faces of the crowd in the court were beginning to show annoyance. Did Potter's lawyer mean to throw away his client's life without any effort at all?

Several more witnesses talked of Potter's guilty behaviour when he reached the scene of the murder the next morning. They too were allowed to leave without being cross-examined about their evidence. Those in the courthouse were extremely puzzled by the behaviour of Potter's lawyer.

With the last of the witnesses heard, the prosecution lawyer stood up. "The prosecution has established the defendant's guilt without any doubt," he said. "We rest our case."

A groan escaped from poor Potter. He put his face in his hands and rocked his body softly to and fro. A pained silence had descended on the court.

Slowly, ever so slowly, Potter's lawyer got to his feet. "Your Honour," he began, looking up at Judge Thatcher. "I had indicated that we would seek mercy on the grounds that Muff Potter did this deed while under the influence of the demon drink. But we have changed our minds. Mr. Potter now pleads not guilty."

What drama! The surprised onlookers could not believe it. Why had Potter suddenly decided to fight the case?

Potter's lawyer now called his only witness. "Call Thomas Sawyer!" he boomed out.

Chapter 19
Tom's Evidence

Tom entered the courtroom and took his place on the stand. The boy looked terrified as he gave the oath and promised to tell the whole truth, and nothing but the truth.

"Thomas Sawyer, where were you at midnight on the seventeenth day of June?" asked Potter's lawyer.

Tom glanced at Injun Joe's face. His throat dried up and the words refused to come. The audience waited for his answer and he felt as if they were willing him to speak. At last he found the strength to answer the lawyer's question.

"On the night of the seventeenth of June," Tom stuttered nervously, "I was in the graveyard, sir."

The court fell as quiet as Hoss Williams' grave.

"So you were you near Hoss Williams grave?" asked Potter's lawyer.

"I was in the graveyard, sir."

"Yes, sir."

"Speak a trifle louder please, Thomas."

"I was as near to the grave," said Tom, "as I am to you now."

"Were you hiding or not?" asked Potter's lawyer.

"I was hiding," answered Tom.

"Where exactly were you hiding?"

"Behind a tombstone, real close to the grave," said Tom.

Injun Joe gave a barely perceptible start.

"Was anyone with you?" asked the lawyer.

"Yes, I went there with Huck Finn."

"And tell me, Thomas," continued the lawyer, "what did you see and hear?"

Tom began, hesitatingly at first, but then he warmed to his subject. Every eye in the room was on him, including Injun Joe's.

The tension was unbearable as Tom got to the end of his tale. "And as Potter was felled by the doctor with the headboard," he said, "I saw Injun Joe jump at the doctor with his knife . . ."

Quick as lightning, and before Tom could say another word, Injun Joe sprang to his feet, raced down the courtroom aisle and vanished through the door!

Injun Joe raced out of the courtroom.

The truth about what had happened to make Muff Potter change his guilty plea emerged soon after. Tom had become too horrified at the thought of sending an innocent man to the gallows. So, despite Huck insisting they should keep quiet, Tom told Potter's lawyer the true story of what had really happened in the grave-yard that fatal night.

Tom became a bit of a hero for saving Potter's life. But Tom was absolutely terrified in case Injun Joe found him. The true murderer haunted all his worst nightmares. And nothing could persuade him to leave the house for any night adventures now.

Huck was in a similar state of terror. They both felt that they wouldn't be safe until they had personally seen Injun Joe's dead corpse. Large rewards were offered for Joe's capture. But, despite the sheriff and his men scouring the country, no sign of him was found.

Time passed and with each new day Tom relaxed a little more. He began to feel safe again.

Chapter 20
Treasure Hunting

There comes a time in every young boy's life when he goes treasure hunting. The idea came to Tom one day when he had run out of mischievous things to do.

He couldn't find his best friend, Bill Harper, so he teamed up with Huckleberry Finn.

"Where'll we dig?" asked Huck.

"Oh, 'most anywhere," replied Tom.

"Why? Is treasure hid everywhere?" asked Huck.

"Sometimes," nodded Tom. "But mostly it's hid on islands, in rotten sea chests, under dead trees or under the floorboards in haunted houses."

"And who hides all this treasure?" asked Huck.

"Why, robbers, of course," said Tom. "Who'd you reckon? Sunday school teachers?"

"If it was mine," said Huck, "I'd spend it and have a good time."

"So would I," agreed Tom. "But robbers don't do it that way. They always hide it."

"Do they come back for it?" asked Huck.

"Not often," was the reply. "And that's why there's a lot of treasure lying about. It's because robbers sometimes forget where they hid it. Or because they died in prison and no one else knew where it was hid."

"Well," said Huck, "we've been on Jackson Island and never found a cent. Perhaps we should find somewhere else to hunt."

"There are lots of places we could try," said Tom. "Let's just head out and see what we find."

So the two boys set out with a shovel and a pick. On the way, they discussed what they would do with all the treasure they found.

"I think I'll have a glass of cream soda every day," said Huck. "And go to every circus that comes along."

"Me, I'll get me a new drum, a sword, a red necktie, a smart pup, and get married to my sweetheart," said Tom.

"Get married!" cried Huck. "Tom, you ain't in your right mind."

"Wait, and you'll see," replied Tom.

"I reckon that's the most foolish thing you

Setting out with a shovel and a pick.

could do," Huck said. "Look at my pa and ma. They fought all the time until they died."

"The girl I'm going to marry," said Tom, "won't fight."

"Just you think a bit more about it," said Huck. "Girls are all the same. Anyway, what's the name of the gal you want to marry?"

"She ain't a gal," said Tom, avoiding the question. "She's a girl."

"Gal or girl," laughed Huck, "they're the same."

They found a likely spot and started digging. By lunchtime, they had dug quite deep holes but found nothing.

"Do robbers always bury things this deep?" asked Huck.

"Sometimes. Not always though," said Tom. "I reckon we haven't got the right place."

So they chose a new spot and started again. They dug until teatime and again found nothing.

"Why don't we try the old ghost house?" suggested Tom. "Everyone knows that robbers like ghosts to protect their treasure."

"Bit spooky," said Huck. "But we can come back tomorrow."

So it was agreed. The next day they were up

bright and early. It was a long walk and they didn't get there until lunchtime.

The house stood on its own in a deserted valley. It hadn't been lived in for years. Its fences had all fallen down, the chimney was leaning at a steep angle and part of the roof had caved in.

Huck had never seen such a miserable place in his life. And Tom distinctly heard spirits whispering in the bushes, and ghosts crying in the trees. A wild dog howled in the distance. Apart from that, all was eerily silent.

They chose their spot some distance from the cottage and started digging. As they dug, Tom told Huck the story of Robin Hood.

"He lived in Sherwood Forest in England. He was the greatest robber that ever lived. He robbed the rich to give to the poor."

"Now that's what I call a noble robber!" said Huck.

"No one could match him in archery," said Tom. "If he had been an American, he could have split a dime in half with an arrow fired from two hundred yards away."

Huck was mighty impressed with the stories of Robin Hood. In fact, because they found no treasure in the holes they dug, they spent most

The house hadn't been lived in for years.

of that afternoon playing Robin Hood in Sher-wood Forest.

It was only later that they decided to go and look into the old house itself. They were so frightened that they tiptoed through the front door. They found themselves in what was the old parlour. The place was very dark and the ceiling was covered with cobwebs. They both jumped as an owl whooshed from the chimney and out of the door.

Suddenly, they heard the sound of footsteps and muffled voices. Someone had just entered the house by the back door.

Tom began to shake with fear. He recog-nised one of the voices. It was Injun Joe's!

Chapter 21
A Plan to Rob Widow Douglas

Tom and Huck crept upstairs as silently as two ghosts. A few moments later, the boys were looking down through a hole in the floor. They saw two figures enter the house.

Tom recognised the first man. He'd seen him in town a few times recently. As far as Tom knew, he was a deaf and dumb Mexican, whose swarthy looks were half hidden by his flowing white hair, whiskers, spectacles, and a large sombrero hat.

The second man was a stranger to both boys. He was a ragged, unkempt fellow.

But where was Injun Joe?

"I don't like it," the unkempt man was saying to the Mexican. "It's dangerous."

To Tom and Huck's surprise the "deaf and dumb" man replied.

"Dangerous!" he grunted. "You've gone soft!"

The voice made both boys gasp and quake.

It was Injun Joe who was hiding in disguise beneath the sombrero.

"Yes, there's danger in the job, Jem," he said, "but I've spied it all out. We'll be alright. We'll be in and out of Widow Douglas' place in minutes. We'll be on our way to Texas before she knows her money is gone. Now let's get back to the village. And bring my bullion box. We don't want to leave my well-earned treasure here."

Both Tom and Huck knew how rich Widow Douglas was. Her late husband had been a lawyer.

Soon after, the two men left the house, carrying a very heavy bullion box. "Keep your eyes open for those boys," said Injun Joe, as he walked away. "I saw 'em playing not far from here yesterday."

"Little devils," said the other man.

"I'll have my revenge on that Sawyer kid before we leg it to Texas," replied Injun Joe. "You see if I don't. He'll wish he'd kept his mouth shut!"

Tom and Huck watched the two men disappear down the hill. As soon as they were out of sight, the boys took a circular route back to the village and went to see the sheriff. They told

It was Injun Joe in disguise!

him all they had heard about the plan to rob Widow Douglas.

"You leave this with me," said the sheriff.

Late that night, Tom was still wide awake when he heard the sound of gunfire. It went on for several minutes and then all was silent.

The next day the news quickly flashed around the village. The sheriff's men had surprised Injun Joe and Jem just as they were breaking into Widow Douglas' home. There had been a fierce gunfight and Jem had been caught. But once again, slippery Injun Joe had escaped. The sheriff had sent out a posse of men to find his trail.

The first thing Tom did that morning was to hurry around to see the sheriff. "Please don't tell anyone that it was me who told you what Injun Joe was planning," he begged. "He's already sworn revenge on me for saving Muff Potter from the gallows."

"All right," said the sheriff. "But you ought to have the credit for what you did."

Tom thanked the sheriff. The boy didn't want any more fame or glory until Injun Joe was long dead and buried.

The sheriff's posse spent a week searching for Injun Joe without seeing a sign of him

131

anywhere. The villain had disappeared once again.

***

There was some good news for poor Tom. Becky Thatcher was back from her holiday overseas. One of the first things that the pair did after she got back was to join a village picnic outing to some famous underground caves, a few miles outside the village.

About thirty people joined the ferry for the journey down the Mississippi to reach the caves. Bundles of candles were produced and lit, before they entered the hauntingly beautiful labyrinth of high-roofed caverns and narrow tunnels. It was said that a man could wander for days in there and still not see all of it.

The party spent two hours wandering around the place. Most people stayed close to the well-marked paths. But Tom, who knew the place better than anyone, spirited Becky away into the furthest nooks and crannies of the caves.

They romantically marked their names on an overhanging rock with the smoke from their

Marking their names on an overhanging rock.

candles before continuing on ever deeper. Eventually they came to a place where a stream of water flowed over a ledge.

Tom squeezed himself between a rock face and the ledge to show Becky the beauty of the rocks far below. Then he saw a tunnel he hadn't been down before. So on they went, deeper and deeper, here and there leaving a smoky mark on the rocks so they could find their way back.

After creeping down the tunnel for several minutes, they found themselves in a great cavern with a huge lake stretching away from them, far beyond the power of the candlelight. The lights from their candles sparkled on great frozen spikes of water.

Becky was a little frightened. "I think we should go back," she said.

Suddenly a cloud of bats, disturbed by the sudden arrival of two humans in their lonely lair, flew into the air above Tom and Becky's heads.

"Yes, we'd better go back," said Tom. "I think even I'm beginning to get a little lost."

They started to retrace their steps, but nothing looked familiar any more. Tom tried to keep Becky's spirits up, but she saw the anxiety in his candlelit eyes.

"Listen!" he suddenly said.

They both listened, hoping to hear some sign of the others. There was nothing but silence.

"Hello!" cried Tom.

The call went echoing down the cold, empty passages, and died away in the distance with a ripple of strange mocking laughter.

Chapter 22
Lost!

Becky burst into tears. "We're lost, aren't we Tom. Why did we leave the others?"

"Becky, I'm such a fool," he replied, sitting down and putting his arm around her. She buried her face in his chest.

"We mustn't lose hope," he said. "We'll find a way out. Even if we don't, someone will find us."

They got up and moved on again. Soon after, Tom took Becky's candle and blew it out. "We must save the light," he explained. "We can see enough with my one candle."

They scrambled on, up and down passages and over dangerous ledges. They could find no trace of the smoke marks they had left on their way down.

Becky was soon exhausted and they stopped again. This time as they rested, she fell asleep in Tom's arms. When she awoke she was so angry with herself. "How could I go to sleep at a time like this!" she cried.

Becky fell asleep in Tom's arms.

"The rest did you good," said Tom. "Now we'll go and find our way out."

They set off again. A long time after that – they had no idea how long – they came upon a spring of fresh water flowing from a tiny hole in a rock. Becky drank a few mouthfuls to refresh herself. So did Tom.

Both of them were exhausted now. "Tom, I'm so hungry," whimpered Becky. Tom searched through his pockets and found a piece of cake he'd saved from tea the day before. He divided the cake and they each had half.

"They will hunt for us, won't they?" asked Becky.

"Of course they will," replied Tom. "They're probably hunting for us right now."

Tom looked down at his candle. It was almost finished. The only piece of candle left now was Becky's.

"Sshh!" said Becky suddenly. "Do you hear something?"

Both held their breath and listened. There was a sound like the faintest far-off shout. Instantly Tom shouted back, and leading Becky by the hand, set off in the direction of the noise.

Setting off in the direction of the noise.

After a while, they stopped and listened again. They heard the same sound. It was getting closer. Tom shouted out again. "Hello!"

"It must be them," said Tom. "They're coming. Come on Becky. We're all right now."

But the more they hurried towards the sound, the fainter it became. Then it was no more.

Tom was desperate now. He decided to explore any passage he hadn't been in yet. He left Becky, promising her that he would keep contact by calling back regularly. He went up and down various passages without finding any clues to the way out.

At last, Tom spotted a ray of light. It grew bigger and more powerful. Someone was walking towards him. And then, just twenty yards away, he saw a flickering candle.

"Hello!" Tom shouted.

The candle came nearer. A shape appeared behind it. Tom froze. It was Injun Joe! So this was where he had been hiding!

Chapter 23
Trapped in the Caves

Injun Joe took one look at the shadowy figure of Tom and scurried away into the darkness like an escaping rat. In his hurry to get away, he dropped his candle. Tom picked it up. It would give him a few more minutes of light.

Tom returned to Becky, who wanted to know why he had called out. Tom just told her that he thought he'd heard voices again.

"There wasn't anyone," he said, "but I did find this candle."

"Thank heavens," said Becky. "I'd die if I was left in the dark down here."

"We'll just have to wait for someone to find us," sighed Tom. "It won't be long."

Tom and Becky fell asleep again. When they awoke, they had lost all track of time. It felt as if they had been underground for days.

Tom was sure it must be Wednesday, Thursday or even Friday by then. They were both tortured with a raging hunger. Becky was

Injun Joe scurried away.

despondent. She was convinced they were both going to die. She made Tom promise that he would stay beside her and hold her hand until it was all over.

Tom, starving and filled with forebodings of doom, kissed her. He hardly dare leave her now, yet he knew that their only hope of survival was for him to find a way out. It was clear to him that the search for them must have been given up long ago.

It was then that he had an idea. He had an old fishing line in his pocket. He knew that it must be at least a few hundred feet long.

"I'm going to leave you for a short while," he told Becky, "but I'll still be beside you in a way."

He tied one end of the line around Becky's waist and then began to unwind the line. "I'm going to find a way out, but I'll tug on the line every now and again so you know I'm okay. I can't get lost if you're holding one end of the line."

Becky still didn't want Tom to go. But she knew it was their only hope.

Tom kissed her again and then disappeared into a dark passageway, feeding out the fishing line as he went.

"I'm going to find a way out."

***

A major search had been mounted for the two lost children. It was only after the picnic party had returned to the village that Tom and Becky were found to be missing.

Alarm bells had been sounded in the village and every able-bodied person had gathered to join a search party. The ferry was ordered into service. Within an hour of the two youngsters going missing, nearly a hundred men and women were pouring down high road and river, towards the caves.

Over the next two days every inch of the known extent of the caves was searched. The names of Becky and Tom were found traced on an overhanging rock with candle smoke. But that was all.

The underground streams in the cave complex were running high. Gradually, the searchers began to think that perhaps the pair had been washed away by a torrent. On the third day of the search, most people sadly returned to the village. The hunt was called off.

Becky's mother was certain that she would never see her daughter again, and all the villagers thought they had seen the last of their hero, Tom Sawyer. Had he not masterminded the stealing of Mr. Dobbin's wig? Had he not saved Muff Potter from the gallows? And had he not saved Widow Douglas from a terrible robbery?

Now Tom Sawyer was no more. They were sure of that.

Chapter 24
Welcome Home

Tom, firmly gripping his fishing line, took an upwards path through a steep tunnel. Inch by inch, he fed out the line. He was worried it would soon run out. But it gave Becky great comfort when he tugged it to show her he was alright. Tom didn't feel quite so alone either, when she tugged the line in return.

Higher and higher he climbed. And suddenly the line grew tight. Tom had gone as far as he could while still staying in contact with Becky. Then he saw it. Just ahead was the tiniest chink of light.

He tied the fishing line to a large rock and crept on down an ever-narrowing tunnel. All the time, the speck of light was growing larger. He could smell fresh air too.

Finally, with his body almost pinned by the rock walls on either side, he squeezed himself out into a small cavern. And there was the source of the light; daylight filtered down from a hole in the roof.

Tom clambered up and poked his head out of the hole. To his utter surprise, he found himself looking down on the great Mississippi River. He cleared away some of the rocks around the hole and climbed out onto the banks of the river.

Tom didn't wait there long. He hurried back to Becky. "We're saved," he cried. "I've found the way out."

It was early evening by the time they both emerged from the caves.

"It's funny," said Tom, "but I don't even recognise this spot on the Mississippi. I haven't a clue where we are."

Just then, they heard a horse and cart close by. They ran up the riverbank and found a farm boy driving a cart.

"Where are we?" asked Tom.

"By the Mississippi of course," the boy replied.

"Are we far from the entrance to the caves?" asked Tom.

"You're at least five miles away," replied the boy. "But wait a minute. Ain't you Tom and Becky?"

Daylight came from a hole in the roof.

"Yes," said Tom.

"My goodness," said the boy. "You've come back from the dead. Everyone thought you were dead and drowned."

The boy immediately offered to take them home.

***

The last rays of the sun were setting when Tom and Becky finally reached the edge of St. Petersburg. News of their return began to spread from house to house. Excited people burst from their homes to welcome back the couple.

It wasn't long before the church bells rang out in celebration. Soon, Tom and Becky were surrounded by just about the entire population of St. Petersburg.

"They've been found!" people cried out. "It's a miracle!"

The rattling of tin pans and the sounding of horns were added to the din as the entire village followed Tom and Becky to Aunt Polly's house.

Aunt Polly was delirious with happiness when she saw Tom. So were Becky's parents when the young girl was finally taken home,

Excited villagers welcomed them back.

too. Tom, of course, took it all without blinking an eyelid. He was a hero yet again.

Later, Tom lay on the sofa in his aunt's parlour and revealed all that had happened to an eager audience, using his ever-vivid imagination to fill in what he thought were the duller bits of the story.

But nearly four days of fear and hunger were not to be shaken off in a matter of hours, as Tom and Becky were to discover. Both children were put to bed with fevers.

Tom stayed in his bed for several days, but there was always a constant stream of visitors. Huck Finn was one of the first to come. Widow Douglas also came to thank him for saving her from being robbed.

Finally Tom was allowed to get up, and he went straight around to Becky's house to see how she was. Becky's father greeted him. Becky was still in bed, but recovering quickly. She smiled warmly on seeing her hero again.

Afterwards, Becky's father said that since the pair had been found, they had erected a strong wooden door at the entrance to the caves. "And I have the key," he added. "It's just to make sure that no one else finds their way into the caves and gets lost."

Welcome Home

Tom's face turned as white as a sheet.

"What's the matter?" asked Becky's father.

"I've just remembered!" Tom exclaimed. "Injun Joe! Injun Joe was hiding in the caves! I saw him!"

Chapter 25
The Fate of Injun Joe

The ferry boat was crowded again as another search party set off for the caves. Tom was beside Judge Thatcher as he took out his key and unlocked the new door guarding the entrance to the caves.

A terrible sight met their eyes. Injun Joe lay stretched out on the ground, dead, with his face close to the crack of the door. It was as if his desperate eyes had been fixed on the light outside.

Injun Joe had been trapped behind the door when he breathed his last. A big knife lay close by, its blade broken in two. The man had been trying to chip and hack his way through the door. He had starved to death!

Tom did feel a little sorrow for the way Injun Joe had died. Yet that feeling was quickly drowned by the sense of relief that the demon had now left this world – and Tom's life – at last.

A terrible sight met their eyes.

Injun Joe was buried near the entrance to the caves. And in times ahead, people flocked to the site in boats and wagons to see the grave. They brought their children too. Mothers warned them that they might end up in that grave with Injun Joe if they got lost in the caves.

***

Gradually, things returned to normal in St. Petersburg. But all this time Huckleberry Finn had been thinking about one thing. Where was Injun Joe's bullion box?

One morning, he went to see Tom. "I've been a thinkin'," he said. "Remember Injun Joe's bullion box? Remember how he took it away with him when he left the old haunted house?"

"Yup," said Tom, with growing excitement.

"Well, I reckon I know where it is. It came to me sudden like. There's only one place it could be."

"Where?" replied Tom.

"Simple," said Huck. "If Injun Joe was hiding out in the caves, then that's where his money is hiding too! What do you say? Shall we go and find it?"

"You bet we will!" cried Tom.

It was as if all Tom's nightmare memories of the caves had vanished in a jiff.

"And if we don't find it," said Huck, "then you can have all my worldly possessions."

"All right," laughed Tom. "It's a whiz! When'll we go?"

"At dawn tomorrow," said Huck.

"Tomorrow it is!" Tom cried. "Another adventure. Perhaps I'll be a hero again! We won't need Judge Thatcher's key, either. We can get in by the hole near the river I discovered."

Preparing for their expedition.

That night the two adventurers prepared for their expedition. They filled their bags with boxes of candles and lumps of chalk to mark their progress, and make sure they didn't get lost.

They knew they could find plenty of water, but they raided Aunt Polly's pantry for food to take with them. Tom told Aunt Polly that he was going to stay with Huck for a few days. She didn't mind at all.

"But make sure you don't go anywhere near those caves," she warned him.

"Never again!" promised Tom with a mischievous smile.

His smile told Aunt Polly that life would never be peaceful when that young rascal was out and about.

Tom was out of the house before first light the next morning, and on his way to meet Huck on the road out of the village.

Chapter 26
Down in the Caves Again

When Tom and Huck reached the caves, they borrowed a small boat to take them upriver to the place from where Tom and Becky had finally escaped.

The first thing that Tom did on seeing his escape hole was to cut some branches from nearby trees and make a rough door for the entrance. Then he covered the branches with grass and twigs. He wanted to keep the place secret.

"There!" he said. "No one else can find that hole now. It will be our secret. You keep mum about it, Huck."

Huck duly promised to keep the secret.

"I've always wanted to be a robber," said Tom, "but you can't be a robber unless you have a cave to hide the loot in. And we don't want people stealing our loot, do we?"

"No, we don't," agreed Huck.

"We'll let Bill Harper in on the secret," said

He wanted to keep the place secret.

Tom, "because you can't have a gang unless you've got more than two people. Tom Sawyer's gang! Sounds splendid, doesn't it, Huck?"

"It sure does," said Huck, "but who'll we rob?"

"'Most anybody really," said Tom. "We'll waylay anyone we find. That's generally the way robbers do it."

"And kill them too?" asked Huck.

"No, not always," replied Tom. "We'll ransom most of them. We can hide them in the cave until we've got the money. But if we ransom women, then we've got trouble. They'll fall in love with us and won't want to leave us. Anyway, that's what happens in all the books."

Huck thought he'd rather be a pirate.

"Well, we're going to be robbers today," said Tom. "We're after Injun Joe's loot."

At last they entered the caves, quickly reaching the spring where Tom and Becky had made their last stop. Tom felt a shudder as he showed Huck the place where Becky had waited for him.

Huck began to feel the dread atmosphere of the place. "Tom, let's git out of here."

"What! And leave the loot?"

"Yes, leave it," said Huck. "Injun Joe's ghost is around here. I'm certain of it."

"His ghost ain't here," said Tom. "It's five miles away at the main entrance. That's where he died, and that's where his ghost will be."

"No Tom," shivered Huck, "a ghost would hang around the money. You and I both know that."

"Oh come on, Huck," pleaded Tom. "We're probably almost sitting on the loot now. It has to be nearby."

Huck reluctantly followed Tom a little deeper along the passage down which Injun Joe had vanished. The rock walls, reflecting the pale light of the candles, seemed to close in on them as they advanced.

It was no illusion. The passage was getting narrower and narrower. Soon there was hardly enough space for Tom and Huck to squeeze through. Huck was now terrified they would be stuck there forever. But just before he finally panicked and fled, Tom called out. "There's something just ahead!"

A few more feet, and Tom and Huck tumbled into a small circular cavern. It was a dead end. If the old haunted cottage in the valley was one of Injun Joe's hideaways, this was certainly another. There was a small bed, with a box of candles beneath it. There was also a small table. Tom guessed this was where Injun Joe had eaten his last meal.

Tom and Huck both looked under the table at the same time. There was the bullion box. It wasn't locked. Tom opened the lid. Inside were two guns, some bullets, a bag of gunpowder and four bulging bags.

"We've found it!" cried Tom.

"We're rich, Tom!" said Huck, opening one of the bags and seeing a huge pile of golden dollars roll out. "But please, Tom, can we git out of this tomb? It's giving me the creeps."

Tom was only too happy to get out now. They left everything behind except the four bags of coins. Squeezing back into the passage, they quickly found their way back to the secret opening. Then they closed the door and hid it with more grass and twigs, before boarding their boat for the journey home.

It was a beautiful evening and all the nightmares of the recent past were now well behind Tom. There was a huge, satisfied smile on his face as he looked towards the moon that was rising into the twilight sky.

The two boys counted all the coins.

"Phew!" gasped Tom. "We're rich!"

"You could knock me over with a feather,

"We're rich, Tom!"

Tom," said Huck, who suddenly felt quite faint.

It was almost dark by the time they got home. They hid the gold in a rusting bucket at the bottom of a disused well. They hadn't planned what to do with their extraordinary fortune yet.

Chapter 27
Two Wealthy Boys

The next evening, Widow Douglas held a party to thank Tom and Huck for their help in alerting the sheriff to Injun Joe's plans to rob her. Everyone was there; Aunt Polly, Sid and Cousin Mary, Becky Thatcher and her parents, Bill Harper, and many others from the village.

There was only one reluctant guest; Huckleberry Finn. Aunt Polly had made him dress up in one of Tom's suits for the occasion. "I ain't used to dressing up," complained Huck. "I don't want to go to any party. I'd rather catch up with some sleep in a haystack. I ain't used to parties and people and things."

But Becky made him come, threatening to send him to school to learn something if he didn't. There was nothing that Huck was more afraid of than the thought of having to learn something. So, dressed more smartly than he'd ever been in his life, Huck did go to the party.

There was only one reluctant guest.

And there, he got another invitation. "Huckle-berry," said Widow Douglas. "I want to give you a reward. I want you to come and live with me. I want to give you a real home. And you can go to school, too."

Huck didn't wait. He fled from the room without even saying goodbye.

"Huck doesn't need a home," Tom said to Widow Douglas, after he had finished laughing. "He doesn't really need educating. That's because he's rich. Huck's real rich. He could afford to buy lots of homes. But he prefers to live in a woodshed most of the time."

Some of the guests started to laugh. How could a vagabond like Huckleberry Finn be rich?

"Perhaps, you don't believe he's rich," said Tom. "But he is. He's got lots of money. I can show you. Just wait a few minutes."

Tom raced out of the house and went to the old well, where he retrieved the four bags of gold coins. They were a huge weight. He staggered all the way back with two bags on each shoulder. He was almost out of breath by the time he entered Widow Douglas' house and dropped the bags on the floor.

Tom opened the bags and poured out their

contents. "There! What did I tell you," he said. "Half of it's mine and the rest is Huck's."

The guests were absolutely astounded to see so many gold coins.

Aunt Polly led the questions. "Where on earth did you find that?" she asked.

For the next hour, Tom held centre stage as he told the whole story. As usual, he added some extra made-up details, to make it even more exciting.

When he had finished, Aunt Polly asked the question everyone wanted to ask. "How much is there?"

"I'm not top of the class at adding," said Tom, "but at a rough guess, twelve thousand dollars."

Even Widow Douglas wasn't that rich!

Tom and Huck's windfall made a mighty stir in the little village of St. Petersburg. So vast a sum, all in cash, seemed next to incredible. It was talked about, gloated over and glorified.

Half the village took to treasure hunting, just in case Injun Joe had left another fortune somewhere. The village newspaper published the whole story on the front page, and inside there were stories about Tom and Huck's lives.

Widow Douglas invested Huck's money

The guests were absolutely astounded.

for him. Judge Thatcher did the same for Tom. Each lad now had a huge income ... a dollar for every weekday of the year and a half on Sundays.

Judge Thatcher had a high opinion of Tom. No ordinary boy would have got his daughter safely out of the caves. And when Becky told her father how Tom had taken the blame – and a whipping – for her in school, he was even more impressed.

The Judge fancied that Tom might become a top lawyer or a great soldier one day.

But taking on anything as boring as a job was the last thing Tom wanted. Now he had money, he could play pirates and Robin Hood any day of the week. And he certainly had no plans to return to school!

Chapter 28
Huck is Free Again

As for Huckleberry Finn, he had escaped from Widow Douglas' grasp at the party. But in the months ahead, she still tried to look after him. Out of politeness, he did try to be looked after. She even introduced him to polite society ... no, dragged him into it, hurled him into it against his will!

The widow's servants kept him clean and neat, combed and brushed. And they put him to bed each night in spotless sheets – at least, when they could find him.

He had to eat with a knife and fork, and use a napkin, cup and plate. He had to learn to read and even go to church.

Huck bravely bore these miseries for a few weeks. Then he went missing.

Widow Douglas hunted for him everywhere. The sheriff mounted a posse to hunt him down. They even dragged the river for his body.

Huck is Free Again

He had to eat with a knife and fork.

173

It was Tom that eventually found him in a neighbour's woodshed. At first Tom urged him to return to Widow Douglas'. But he could see how Huck could never be tamed.

"Don't send me back," said Huck. "I've tried living with Widow Douglas, but Tom, that life ain't for me. I ain't used to it. The widow's good to me and friendly. But she won't let me sleep in the woodshed. She makes me wear Sunday best. I have to ask permission to go fishin', permission to go swimmin'. We eat by the clock. We go to bed by the clock. We do everything by the clock."

Tom interrupted him. "But everybody does things that way."

"I ain't everybody," grumbled Huck. "I'm different. I prefer to sleep in woodsheds. I prefer to dress in rags. And I'll tell you what, bein' rich ain't what's it's cracked up to be. It just makes me worry what to do with all the money. I ain't happy any more. I've made my mind up now . . ."

"To do what?" said Tom.

"You can take all my money. I don't want it. No, I won't be rich! I won't live in a fancy house. I prefer the woods and the rivers. I want to be free again."

"But you'll still be one of my gang, won't you?" asked Tom.

"Yup," smiled Huck. "I'll be as good a pirate and a robber as ever. I'll be better. When did you ever meet a pirate or robber who stayed rich? They always lose their money in the end, just like Injun Joe did."

"All right, Huck," said Tom. "I'll tell Widow Douglas that you send your thanks but want to return to the wild."

"That's my boy," said Huck. "Besides, we haven't sworn on anything recently. Tell you what, let's get together tonight for a grand swearing."

"What'll we swear to?" asked Tom.

"To stand by each other," replied Huck. "To never tell each other's secrets."

"And that swearing's got to be done at exactly midnight," interrupted Tom. "And in the loneliest, most haunted house in all the world."

"Yes!" said Huck. "And we'll need a coffin to swear on. And some blood to write the words with."

"Now that's something to write home about," said Tom. "That's a real whiz!"

And, of course, Tom, Huck Finn, Bill Harper and the rest of their pals became the most

"You'll still be one of my gang, won't you?"

feared gang of pirates and robbers that ever set sail on the great Mississippi River.

But that's a whole new story to be told another day!

The End